W9-BYK-545

My Weird School Special

Bummer in the Summer!

Pictures by
Jim Paillot

Dan Gutman

HARPER

An Imprint of HarperCollinsPublishers

To Emma

My Weird School Special: Bummer in the Summer!
Text copyright © 2019 by Dan Gutman
Illustrations copyright © 2019 by Jim Paillot
information address HarperCollins Children's Books, a division of HarperCollins
Publishers, 195 Broadway, New York, NY 10007.
www.harpercollinschildrens.com

ISBN 978-0-06-279681-3 (pbk. bdg.)–ISBN 978-0-06-279682-0 (library bdg.)

Typography by Laura Mock
19 20 21 22 23   PC/LSCH   10 9 8 7 6 5 4 3 2
❖
First Edition

Contents

Three Months of Recess!

My name is A.J. and I hate ghosts.

Ghosts are creepy! They're always following you around, pestering you, and haunting your house. They like to make scary noises in the middle of the night to freak people out. I guess they have nothing better to do with their time.

When I drop dead someday, I'm not going to bother people or scare them by making noises in the middle of the night. I'm just going to sit around playing video games. That would be a great life. I mean, death.

When I was a little kid, I was sure there was a ghost living in my bedroom closet. I couldn't sleep at night. So my parents took out the vacuum cleaner and sucked up the ghost. It was like *Ghostbusters*! But I never go into my closet anymore. And I'm *never* going to use the vacuum cleaner, because there's a ghost inside it.

Just kidding! I'm a big guy now, and I don't believe in ghosts anymore. I don't know why I started talking about ghosts in the first place. There won't be anything else in this book about ghosts. I promise.

What I *really* want to talk about is the summer. Summer is going to be here soon, and it's my favorite time of the year. Why? Because we don't have to go to school in the summer, of *course*.

Think about it–three whole months with no school! That's about ninety days. I worked it out on a calculator. Ninety days is 2,160 hours; 2,160 hours is 129,600 minutes; 129,600 minutes is 7,776,000 seconds–more than seven *million* seconds! That's a lot of time! And I'm not going to waste any of those seconds.

Summer is still a few months away, but I believe in advance planning. So here's my plan for this coming summer. I wrote it down so I wouldn't forget. . . .

Go swimming.
Eat ice cream.*
Play ball.
Lie in the grass.
Go to the beach.

---

*Do you know what I like to do right after eating ice cream? Eat *more* ice cream!

Catch fireflies.

Watch TV.

Play video games.

Throw Frisbees.

Have water balloon fights.

Play Ping-Pong.

Peel off my sunburned skin.

Eat more ice cream.

Hang out with my friends Ryan, Michael, Neil, and Alexia.

Eat candy.

Sleep late and stay up late.
Eat even more ice cream.

That's what makes a great summer.

I also made a list of stuff I *won't* be doing this summer. . . .

No teachers.
No books or book reports.
No homework.
No reading.
No writing.
No math.
No social studies.
No assemblies.
No lining up in single file.
No Word of the Day.

No cafeteria food.

No report cards.

No rules.

No learning stuff.

No Andrea and no Emily.

No weird grown-ups.

Summer is like three months of recess! Just *thinking* about the summer coming makes me feel happy. This is sure to be the greatest summer of my life. And I'll only have to wait a few months for it to start.

I put on my Superman pajamas and climbed into bed thinking about the great summer ahead. I lay on my back and clasped my hands behind my head, which is what you do when you're feeling happy. Nobody knows why. Life was good. As I dozed off to sleep, I was thinking about the fantastic summer I was going to have.

That's when the weirdest thing in the history of the world happened.

I'm not going to tell you what it was.

Okay, okay, I'll tell you. But you have to read the next chapter. So nah-nah-nah boo-boo on you.

The Underwearwolf

I was fast asleep, which makes no sense at all because you can't be slow asleep, can you? You don't sleep slow or fast. You just sleep at one speed.

There was an empty silence. I opened my eyes. It was dark and spooky outside my bedroom window. I heard the sound of rattling chains. And then, suddenly, there was a light shining through the fog outside. It was a flashlight, I think. That's when the window opened, all by itself.

And then . . . somebody climbed into my bedroom!

"Ahhhhhhhhhh!" I screamed.

It was a boy. He was wearing white underwear and no pants. That was weird. But *everything* about him was weird. He was weighted down by heavy chains. I saw it with my own eyes!* You should have *been* there!

My eyes had to adjust to the light. It was

---

*Well, it would be pretty hard to see something with somebody *else's* eyes.

hard to see. Finally, I figured out who the boy was. It was my friend Billy, who lives around the corner!

"I am the Underwearwolf!" Billy announced. And then he let out an eerie cackling laugh that totally freaked me out. I was trembling with fear. I thought I was gonna die!

"Ahhhhhhhhhh!"

I remembered that Billy dressed up for Halloween last year as the Underwear-wolf. He's basically a werewolf who wears underwear, so he has the perfect name. Billy is weird.

I was sure my mom and dad were going to come running into my room to find out what was going on. But they didn't. I guess they didn't hear anything.

"Billy, you scared me!" I told him. "What are you doing here? It's the middle of the night. Shouldn't you be home, asleep?"

"I come with a warning, A.J.," Billy said in a spooky voice. "You have been a bad boy. A *very* bad boy."

"Wait," I said. "You just broke into my house in the middle of the night dressed up like a monster, and *I've* been a bad boy?"

"That's right," Billy replied.

"What did I do?" I asked.

"I'm not going to tell you," Billy replied. "But you will be haunted by spirits who will come to visit you. You must listen to them, or else."

"Or else *what*?" I asked.

"You'll find out," he replied mysteriously.

"Oh, come on," I told Billy. "That's just crazy."

It was. And to prove it, Billy let out another eerie cackling laugh that sent shivers down my spine. You know some-body's crazy when they let out an eerie cackling laugh for no reason.

"You must believe me, A.J.," Billy said. "The spirits are coming."

"When?" I asked. "When will they be here?"

"Very soon," he replied. "The first one will come . . . in the next chapter!"

"That will be on the next page!" I shouted.

Suddenly the weirdest thing in the history of the world happened. Billy jumped out the window! He made another eerie cackling laugh on his way down.

That was it. He was gone.

I guess it was just a bad dream.

The Ghost of Summer Past

I went back to sleep, thinking that was the end of it. Everybody has a bad dream now and then, right? No big deal. It happens every day.

I was sleeping soundly. I'm not sure if that means I was making a lot of sound or if I wasn't making any sound at all. Anyway, after an hour or two, I heard the clock strike ten. That was weird, because I don't have a clock in my bedroom.

I opened my eyes. The window was closed, but I felt the presence of somebody . . . or something . . . in my room. And then there was this spooky voice. . . .

"A.J. . . . A.J. . . . A.J. . . ."

My name echoed off the walls. Maybe it was my imagination. It could have been a hallucination. Or a dramatization. I'm not sure, because there was very little illumination. My name is an abbreviation. There should have been some elaboration. Or amplification. It was very poor communication. That was my evaluation. For me, it was a humiliation. I just hoped it wasn't an assassination. I should conduct an investigation.

Sorry, I got carried away.*

And then, suddenly, I noticed a fuzzy-looking figure hovering over my bed.

"Ahhhhhhhhhh!"

It was a ghost!

Okay, okay. I know I said there would be nothing else about ghosts in this book. But what was I supposed to do? It was out of my control! The ghost just showed up in my bedroom. You've gotta believe me!

I could see right through the ghost floating in the air. It started forming into

---

*Isn't using big words fun? If you ask me, I should get a standing ovation.

the shape of a person. He was a man. A bald man. His head was glowing like a lightbulb. Actually, he looked a lot like my principal at school, Mr. Klutz. But why would Mr. Klutz be floating over my bed in the middle of the night?

I didn't know what to say. I didn't know what to do. I had to think fast.

"Who are y-you?" I asked in a trembling voice.

"I am the ghost of summers past," he replied, "*Your* past, A.J."

"Oh, yeah?" I said. "I don't believe in ghosts."

"Well, we believe in *you*," the ghost replied.

"You look a lot like the principal at my school, Mr. Klutz," I told the ghost.

"I bet you say that about *all* the handsome bald-headed ghosts who hover over your bed in the middle of the night," said the ghost of Mr. Klutz.

"Are you one of those spirits that my friend Billy said was going to visit me?" I asked.

"You got that right," replied the ghost of Mr. Klutz.

"What are you doing here?" I asked him. "What do you want with me? I'm trying to sleep. This is a school night, you know."

The ghost of Mr. Klutz held up his hand and made a victory peace sign with his fingers, which means "shut up."

"Come," he said, holding out his floating hand. "Follow me, A.J."

"HUH?" I said, which is also "HUH" backward. I got out of bed. "Follow you where? Where are we going?"

"Out the window," the ghost of Mr. Klutz replied. As he said that, the window opened all by itself.

"B-but . . ."

The ghost of Mr. Klutz giggled.

"What's so funny?" I asked.

"You said 'but,' which sounds just like 'butt' even though it only has one *t* in it."

Well, that was true. They really should have two separate words for "but" and "butt." But it seemed like a pretty immature thing for a man to say.

The ghost of Mr. Klutz floated over to the window.

"Come with me, A.J.," he said. "We're going on a journey."

"Out the window?" I asked. "I don't *think* so. *You* can go out the window. I'm staying right here."

"Don't be afraid, A.J.," the ghost of Mr. Klutz said, floating halfway out the window. "You can fly, just like me."

The ghost of Mr. Klutz was nuts!

"No way," I told him. "I'll fall."

"Hold my hand and you won't fall," he said. "Just take one step. Trust me."

He was all the way out the window now, floating there. I went over to the window.

"I'm scared," I admitted.

"You, scared?" the ghost of Mr. Klutz said. "Isn't that what you're always saying about the girl in your class named Emily?"

"How do *you* know about that?" I asked.

"Oh, I know about *everything* you say and do, A.J.," the ghost of Mr. Klutz replied. "Come. Don't be a crybaby. Take a step out the window and come flying with me."

Nobody calls *me* a crybaby. I put my foot up on the windowsill. Flying sounded cool, even though it was scary.

I leaned out the window.

I put my other foot on the windowsill.

I closed my eyes.

I took a step.

I was floating! I was *flying*!

"WOW!" I said, which is "MOM" upside down. "Am I a ghost too? Am I dead?"

"Temporarily, yes," said the ghost of Mr. Klutz. "Okay, follow me, A.J."

I floated out the window and put my

hands in front of me, like Superman. The ghost of Mr. Klutz led the way. We flew over my house and started gliding over rooftops. I was swooping up, down, left, and right. Flying is probably the coolest thing in the history of the world. If I could choose one superpower over all the others, it would be the power to fly.

We flew a long way, maybe a million hundred miles. Suddenly it wasn't nighttime anymore. It was the middle of the day, and it was hot out. I could see water in the distance. It looked like the ocean.

"Where are we?" I asked.

"We're in the past now," the ghost of Mr. Klutz told me. "It's last summer. Do you

remember last summer, A.J.?"

"Sure," I told him. "My family rented a beach house, and all my friends came over."

"That's right," said the ghost of Mr. Klutz. Suddenly I could see the beach in front of me. It was filled with blankets, coolers, umbrellas, and lots of people playing in the sand and swimming in the ocean.

"Look!" I shouted. "There are my friends Ryan, Michael, Neil, and Alexia playing football on the beach. Hey guys! Look at me, I'm flying!"

"They can't see or hear you, A.J.," the ghost of Mr. Klutz told me. "Remember, this isn't today you're seeing. This is last summer."

"Oh, yeah," I said. "Oooh, look! There's me! And there's Mr. Sunny, the lifeguard. And there's Andrea Young, that annoying girl in my class with curly brown hair!"

We swooped down low. Mr. Sunny was

building a giant sand castle. I remembered that he loved everything to do with sand. Andrea was staring at him and making goo-goo eyes. She had a crush on Mr. Sunny. The ghost of Mr. Klutz and I were flying so low that I could hear Andrea talking to A.J. in the past.

"I have it all planned out," Andrea said. "When I grow up, Mr. Sunny and I will be married right here on the beach. We'll have a solar-powered bungalow, and I'll help him build sand castles all day. It will be *sooooooo* romantic."

"You can't marry Mr. Sunny, dumbhead," A.J. in the past told Andrea. "He's too old for you."

"You're mean, Arlo!" Andrea shouted at A.J. in the past. "I can marry anybody I want!"

"Dumbhead!" A.J. in the past shouted at Andrea.

The ghost of Mr. Klutz swooped up in the air and I followed him.

"That wasn't very nice, A.J.," he told me. "Why do you say mean things like 'dumbhead' to Andrea all the time?"

"She says mean things to *me*," I replied.

"Two wrongs don't make a right," said the ghost of Mr. Klutz. "Come, A.J. Let's go to another place."

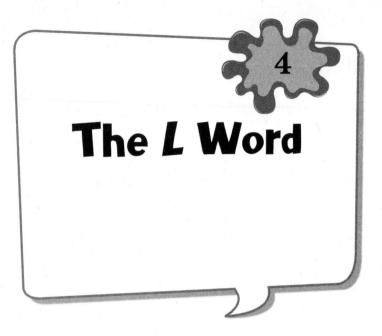

The *L* Word

I followed the ghost of Mr. Klutz as we swooped higher into the sky. Then we zoomed really fast away from the ocean.

"Where are you taking me *now*?" I asked.

"You'll find out," the ghost of Mr. Klutz replied.

Flying is so cool. I wish I could fly everywhere. We swooped down lower, and I could see the rooftop of Ella Mentry School in the distance. That's my school.

"Wait, you're taking me to *school*?" I asked.

"Yes," the ghost of Mr. Klutz replied, "in more ways than one."

We were getting closer to the school.

The ghost of Mr. Klutz wasn't slowing down.

It looked like we were going to crash right into the wall of the school!

"Watch out!" I shouted, putting my hands over my eyes.

But we didn't crash. We flew right

through the wall! It was the coolest thing *ever*. Being a temporary ghost was fun!

The ghost of Mr. Klutz and I flew through the wall into the vomitorium. It used to be called the cafetorium, but then some first grader threw up in there and everybody started calling it the vomitorium. It was all decorated for Halloween, with pictures of witches and pumpkins and bats and stuff.*

The whole gang was sitting below us eating lunch, including me, A.J. in the past.

"Can they see or hear us?" I asked the ghost of Mr. Klutz.

---

*What are you looking down here for? The story's up there.

"No," he replied as we hovered over the table. "Do you remember this day, A.J.?"

"Oh, yeah," I replied. "Halloween is my favorite holiday."

"Do you *love* it?" the ghost of Mr. Klutz asked me.

Ugh, he said the *L* word. I didn't answer. I try to never say the *L* word out loud. That's the first rule of being a kid.

"Wait a minute," I said. "I thought you were the ghost of SUMMERS past."

"Halloween isn't in the summer?" asked the ghost of Mr. Klutz. "Oops. I really need to get a calendar."

Below us, my friends were talking about Miss Mary, who was a student teacher and also happens to be Mr. Klutz's daughter.

"Miss Mary is scary," A.J. in the past said.

"She looks like a vampire," said Neil.

"Maybe she really *is* a vampire," said A.J. in the past. "Did you ever think of that? She dresses in all black. She wears black makeup. She's got a pet bat."

"Stop trying to scare Emily," Andrea told A.J. in the past.

"I'm scared," said Emily.

"Miss Mary probably lives in a cave and sleeps hanging upside down from the ceiling," said A.J. in the past. "Then she goes out at night and bites people in the neck and drinks their blood."

"We've got to *do* something!" Emily

yelled, and then she went running out of the vomitorium. Everybody laughed except Andrea, who made a mean face at A.J. in the past.

The ghost of Mr. Klutz turned to me.

"That wasn't very nice, A.J. The things you said that day weren't nice to Emily, and it wasn't nice what you said about my daughter either."

"I was just trying to be funny," I told him.

"Sometimes what's funny to you isn't funny to other people," the ghost of Mr. Klutz told me. "Sometimes what's funny to you hurts other people's feelings."

"What if I say I'm sorry?" I asked.

"It's too late now," said the ghost of Mr. Klutz. "That happened a long time ago. Let's go."

I followed the ghost of Mr. Klutz as he

flew through the wall again and out of the school.

"You seem to have a lot of anger in you, A.J.," the ghost of Mr. Klutz said as we flew over the rooftops. "It's not nice to be a hater."

"I'm not a hater," I told the ghost of Mr. Klutz. "I hate haters."

"Is that so?" he replied, taking a piece of paper out of his pocket as he flew. "I made a little list of things you've said you hate. Let me see. You said you hate school. You said you hate spiders. You hate reading out loud. Tests. Snot. Ferrets. Germs. Being smart. Putting on plays. Board games. Taking a bath. Flowers. Rain—"

"Yeah, I guess I did say I hate those things," I admitted.

"—Getting hit by water balloons," the ghost of Mr. Klutz continued. "Coffee. Dead fish. When a helicopter falls on your head. Zombies. When the school gets attacked by monsters. Toilet seats. When an alien spaceship lands in the middle of the playground. When an asteroid crashes into the earth and wipes out all life on our planet—"

"Yeah, I said I hate that stuff too, come to think of it," I admitted.

"Okay, so I know lots of things that you hate," the ghost of Mr. Klutz said. "Now tell me some of the things that you *love.*"

He said the *L* word again!

"I don't *L anything.*"

"Are you telling the truth, A.J.?" the ghost of Mr. Klutz asked me.

"Of *course* I'm telling the truth!"

"If you're not telling the truth," the ghost of Mr. Klutz said, "that would make you a hater *and* a liar."

"I never told a lie in my life," I insisted.

"Oh no?" said the ghost of Mr. Klutz. "You said there would be no ghosts in this book, and here I am. So that was a lie."

"Hey, I didn't know you were going to show up!" I shouted at him. I was really mad now. "I'm innocent!"

"I think you might have an anger management problem, A.J.," the ghost of Mr. Klutz told me. "It would be good if you could appreciate some of the *nice* things in life. All the things that you love."

Ugh. He said that word *again*.

"I bet there are lots of things that you

love, A.J." said the ghost of Mr. Klutz.

"The *L* word is for girls," I told him.

"Love is for *everybody*, A.J.," he replied. "Admit it!"

"No!"

We were getting close to my house.

"It's time for you to go back home now," the ghost of Mr. Klutz told me as we hovered outside my window. "As you mentioned, it's a school night."

"Can't we fly around some more?" I asked. "Flying is awesome."

"Will you admit that you *love* flying, A.J.?"

I didn't want to say the *L* word out loud. I didn't know *what* to say. I didn't know what to do. I had to think fast. This was the worst thing to happen since TV Turnoff Week.

But I couldn't say it. I wasn't going to say the *L* word. So I didn't say anything.

"Good night, A.J.," said the ghost of Mr. Klutz with a sigh.

I climbed back through the window and got into bed. I turned around to say good-bye, but the ghost of Mr. Klutz was already gone.

I touched my skin. I wasn't a ghost anymore. I pulled the covers up over my head and went back to sleep.

This was turning out to be a *very* weird night. And it was about to get weirder.

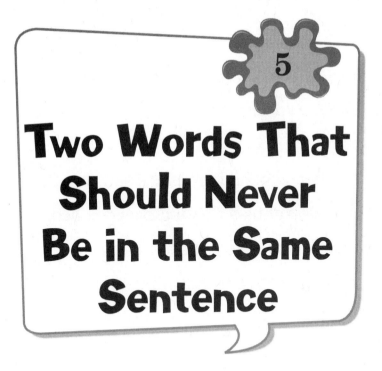

Two Words That Should Never Be in the Same Sentence

I thought that was the end of it. Seeing the ghost of Mr. Klutz had to be just a once-in-a-lifetime bad dream. Nothing like that could ever happen again.

But then something *else* weird happened. The clock struck eleven, and I thought I should really get myself a clock.

Just as I was falling back asleep, I heard another spooky voice.

"A.J. . . . A.J. . . . A.J. . . ."

When I opened my eyes, I saw that there were *two* ghosts floating over my bed.

"Ahhhhhhhhhh!" I screamed.

The ghosts put their fingers up to their lips.

"Shhhhhhh," they whispered.

"Help!" I shouted. "Security! There's somebody in my room!"

"Shhhhhhh."

"What are you doing in my bedroom?" I asked. "How did you get in here? Isn't this breaking and entering?"

The words READ LIKE CRAZY were

on the ghosts' shirts, and the ghosts were each carrying a big cardboard box. I looked at the ghosts more closely. They looked a lot like Mr. Macky, our reading specialist, and Mrs. Roopy, our librarian.

"Mrs. Roopy?" I called out. "Mr. Macky?"

"Never heard of those people," said the ghost that looked like Mrs. Roopy. "We are . . . the ghosts of summer reading."

WHAT?! "Summer" and "reading" are two words that should never be in the same sentence. That's the first rule of being a kid.

"I never heard of the ghosts of summer reading," I said.

"It's a thing," said Mr. Macky.

"You two look *just* like Mr. Macky and Mrs. Roopy from my school."

"We get that all the time," said the ghost of Mr. Macky.

"We brought you some presents, A.J.," said the ghost of Mrs. Roopy.

Presents? I like getting presents! Maybe these weren't bad ghosts. I wondered what was in the boxes they were carrying. The ghosts floated down and put them on the edge of my bed.

"Is there a new video game system in there?" I asked excitedly. "Is it a new skateboard?"

"No," said Mr. Macky. "We brought you some . . . books."*

---

*Betcha didn't see *that* coming!

WHAT!? Books?! I hate books! I don't even know why you're reading *this* one. Books are boring. Reading is boring.

"I don't like to read," I told the two ghosts.

They let out eerie cackling laughs as they opened the boxes.

"That's too bad," said Mr. Macky, pulling out a thick book and handing it to me. "Because this summer your assignment will be to read *The Complete Works of William Shakespeare*."

"Noooooooo!" I shouted, covering my ears. "Not Shakespeare! He's the most boring of all!"

Mrs. Roopy pulled a fat book out of her box. "This is the first book of a twenty-book encyclopedia," she told me. "You'll have to read all twenty books."

"*Noooooooo!*" I screamed at her. "Not an encyclopedia!"

There was nothing I could do. They were already pulling more books out of their boxes. Fiction. Nonfiction. Chapter books. Nonchapter books. Picture books. Nonpicture books. It was horrible! I wanted to run away to Antarctica and live with the penguins.

"And after that, just for fun," said Mr. Macky, "we're going to have you read a complete collection of all the books that have won the Newbery Medal."

"No, not the Newbery books!" I screamed. "Anything but them! I'll be bored to death!"

"Oh, and by the way," said Mr. Macky, "there will be a test on all these books on the first day of school in September."

"No! No! *Noooooooo!*" I shouted. "I hate reading, and I hate tests! Get out of my bedroom!"

"Have a good summer . . . reading!" said Mrs. Roopy. The two of them broke into another eerie cackling laugh as they flew through the window. I could hear them chanting, "*I* before *E* except after *C* . . . or when sounding like *A* as in 'neighbor' and 'weigh.' *I* before *E* except after *C* . . ."

I lay my head back on the pillow. It was *another* terrible dream. No, not a dream. It was a *nightmare*. This was the worst thing to happen since National Poetry Month. When would I wake up from this awful night? I couldn't wait for morning to come.

Somehow I managed to fall back asleep. But I was tossing and turning the whole time.

Bad News and Worse News

"A.J. . . . A.J. . . . A.J. . . ."

Oh no, not *again*! I had been sleeping peacefully when I heard more voices above my bed. I opened my eyes. This time, there were *three* ghosts floating over me!

"Ahhhhhhhhhh!"

It was Miss Daisy, Mr. Granite, and Mr.

Cooper—all three teachers I've had at Ella Mentry School! I had never seen them together.

"Hello, A.J.," said the ghost of Mr. Granite. "Long time no see."

"Mr. Granite!" I said. "I thought you went back to your home planet."

"I did," he replied. "But I came back here because we have some important news for you."

"What is it?"

"There's bad news and worse news," said the ghost of Miss Daisy. "Which do you want to hear first?"

"This has been a horrible night so far," I told them. "Give me the bad news first."

"You're going to have to repeat third grade," said the ghost of Mr. Cooper.

"What?! I have to do third grade all over again?"

"That's right," the ghost of Mr. Cooper told me.

"Why? What did I do?"

"Let me see," said the ghost of Mr. Cooper. "You talk in class. You shout things out without raising your hand. You don't turn in your homework. You come to school late. . . ."

Hmmm. I couldn't argue with that.

"You're absent too many days," continued the ghost of Mr. Granite. "You go to the bathroom just to get out of class. You put a worm in Emily's sneaker during recess. You wrote KICK ME on a piece of paper and taped it to Andrea's back.* You told Emily she had six toes on each foot. You started a war by shooting rubber bands at the girls' Barbie dolls. You hypnotized Andrea and told her that her feet smell like rotten cabbage. . . ."

---

*I'm just glad he didn't mention the time I hypnotized Andrea and told her that her feet smell like rotten cabbage.

"Should we continue?" said the ghosts of Mr. Cooper and Mr. Granite.

"But I don't *want* to go through third grade all over again!"

"Are you ready for the worse news?" asked the ghost of Miss Daisy.

"No," I groaned.

"Before you go through third grade all over again," she said, "you have to go through second grade all over again. And first grade too. You're going to have to start school all over again from the beginning."

"WHAT?!" I shouted. "No! That's not fair!"

"Sorry," said the ghost of Mr. Granite. "And oh, by the way, from now on, school is going to be all year round. No more summer vacation."

"WHAT?!"

"Yes, the Board of Education changed the schedule," said the ghost of Mr. Cooper. "They found that during summer vacation kids forget much of what they learned during the school year. So the Board of Ed decided to get rid of summer vacation entirely."

Ahhhhhhhhhh!

The Ghost of Now

This was turning out to be the worst night in the history of nights. When would it end? The clock that I didn't have struck one.

"A.J. . . . A.J. . . . A.J. . . ."

"Ahhhhhhhhhhh!"

There was *another* weird-looking ghost

floating over my bed! It took me a few seconds to realize it was the ghost of Dr. Brad, our school counselor. He has crazy hair and looks like one of those mad scientists in the movies who straps people to a chair, removes their brain, and puts a monkey brain in its place.

"I am zee ghost of vut's happening right now," said Dr. Brad.*

He talks funny, and his eyebrows jump up and down as he speaks.

"Wait," I said. "Right now has a ghost? That's weird."

"I vud like you to come vis me, A.J.,"

---

*If you read this book out loud, give Dr. Brad a funny mad scientist voice. It will be hilarious.

said the ghost of Dr. Brad. "Vee are going on a leetle journey."

Another journey? The journey with Mr. Klutz wasn't much fun.

Oh, well, I figured. At least I would get to fly again. Flying is cool.

"When are we going?" I asked.

"Right now, of course," the ghost of Dr. Brad replied. "I am zee ghost of vut's happening right now."

He floated out the window, and I followed him. I wasn't afraid this time.

"Come," said the ghost of Dr. Brad. "Zare is much to see."

We flew about a mile or so, and then we swooped down over a playground.

But it wasn't the playground of my school. It was the playground of Dirk School, another school in our town. The guys and me call it Dork School. It's for really smart kids.

There were lots of kids running around the playground. It must have been their recess time. There were some big posters on the walls with slogans like RESPECT OTHERS and BE CONSIDERATE. The ghost of Dr. Brad and I floated low over the playground.

"Do you notice anyzing different about zis school, A.J.?" he asked me.

"Uh . . . the kids are dorks?" I guessed.

"No," said the ghost of Dr. Brad. "Zuh children are being *nice* to each uhzer."

He was right. Nobody was pushing and fighting or saying mean things to anybody else.

"Zee vut I mean?" said the ghost of Dr.

Brad. "Zuh children are sharing. Zay are cooperating. Zay are helping each other. And zay are having fun, A.J."

Hmmmm, interesting. Everybody at Dirk School seemed so happy.

"Wait," I said. "Are you telling me that kids can actually have a good time without saying mean things to each other?"

"Yes! Zat is exactly vut I am saying."

I had no idea this was possible. I always

thought the only way to have fun was to say dumb stuff about other kids and make everybody else laugh. This was blowing my mind!

"Can I go to Dirk School?" I asked.

"No," said the ghost of Dr. Brad. "Only zuh *nice* boys and girls can come here. But zis is how you are supposed to behave, A.J. People need to be polite and respect-ful of one annozer so zay can live in peace and harmony. You vud never get into zis school. Sorry, A.J."

We flew to my house without saying anything. I went back to bed. The ghost of Dr. Brad had given me somezing to zink about. I mean, something to think about.

More Bad News

The clock struck two.

"A.J. . . . A.J. . . . A.J. . . . A.J. . . . A.J. . . . A.J. . . ."

"Ahhhhhhhhhh!"

I opened my eyes to see that my bedroom was *filled* with ghosts. There must have been seven or eight of them floating around in there!

I recognized Mrs. Yonkers, our computer teacher, and Ms. Leakey, our health teacher. Miss Small, our Fizz Ed teacher, was there. So was Miss Tracy, who came to school to teach us about astronomy. And Miss Newman, the local TV weather lady. There was Mr. Will, the guy who drives

the Ding-Dong ice cream truck. And Mr. Burke, the guy who mows the lawn at school. And Mrs. Lilly, a reporter for the local newspaper.

"We are ghosts," they all said at the same time.

"I kinda figured that," I told them. "What

are you all doing here?"

"I have some bad news, A.J.," said the ghost of Mr. Will.

"Oh great," I groaned. "Who doesn't? What's *your* bad news?"

"I ran out of ice cream today," said the ghost of Mr. Will.

"That's not so bad," I told him. "You can get more ice cream tomorrow."

"No," the ghost of Mr. Will replied. "I'm afraid there's no more ice cream left. There's a worldwide ice cream shortage."

WHAT?!

"How long is the ice cream shortage supposed to last?" I asked.

"Forever," replied the ghost of Mr. Will.

"There's no more candy either," said the

ghost of Ms. Leakey. "It's all gone."

"Nooooooo!" I shouted. "No more ice cream or candy? Those are the two most important food groups! How am I going to survive?"

"Sports have been canceled this summer too," said Miss Small sadly.

"And all the swimming pools have to be drained," said Mr. Burke.

"WHAT?!" I shouted. "No more sports? No swimming either? What happened?"

"We believe it has something to do with the earth's rotation," said Mrs. Yonkers. "I've been tracking it on the computer."

"Perhaps I can explain," said Miss Tracy. "For reasons we don't quite understand, the speed that the earth turns around its axis has sped up in the last few days. What happened was, radiation blah blah gravitation blah blah constellation blah blah calculation blah blah calibration blah blah combination blah blah dehydration blah blah navigation blah blah situation blah blah transformation blah blah. . . ."

I had no idea what she was talking about.

"You see," said Mrs. Newman, "there was a high-pressure blah blah, which caused a thermal inversion vector blah blah, which led to global blah blah and wind chill factor blah blah blah blah."

I had no idea what she was talking about either. But I knew one thing for sure. It was the most horrible thing to happen in the history of the world!

"This is big news!" said Mrs. Lilly, sticking a microphone in my face. "I'm writing a story about it for the newspaper. Do you care to comment, A.J.?"

"Get out of here!" I shouted at all of them. "Get out of my room!"

The ghosts let out eerie cackling laughs before they lined up in single file and flew out the window.*

This was the worst night in the history of my life. I simply could not fall back asleep after everything they said. My life was ruined.

---

*How come all ghosts have an eerie cackling laugh? What's up with that?

Bingle Boo!

9

"A.J. . . . A.J. . . . A.J. . . ."

You'll never believe in a million hundred years whose ghost was hovering over my bed *this* time.

It was Mrs. Kormel, the lady who drives our school bus!*

---

*It was Mrs. Kormel who named Neil "the nude kid." She told us she was going to pick up "the new kid," and we thought she said "the nude kid." That was weird.

"Bingle boo!" the ghost of Mrs. Kormel said.

Oh, yeah. She invented her own secret language. Bingle boo means "hello." Mrs. Kormel is not normal.

"What are *you* doing here?" I asked.

"*Somebody* had to drive all those ghosts over here."

"Get out of my bedroom!" I screamed at her. "Ghosts don't take buses!"

"Sheesh," she said. "Don't take it out on me. You have an anger management problem, you know that?"

How Does It Feel?

The clock struck three.

"A.J. . . . A.J. . . . A.J. . . . ," whispered an annoying, squeaky voice.

Oh no. I opened my eyes. There was *another* ghost floating over my bed. It was a smaller ghost than the other ghosts.

"Guess who, A.J.?" the ghost said in a taunting voice.

"My sister, Amy?" I guessed.

"No," said the ghost. "It's me, Emily!"

"Ahhhhhhhhhh!"

She let out an eerie cackling laugh.

"You thought those *other* ghosts were scary?" the ghost of Emily said. "Well, I'm going to be your worst nightmare, A.J."

"What did I ever do to *you*?" I asked, trembling.

"Are you kidding?" the ghost of Emily asked, getting right in my face. "You've been making fun of me and calling me a crybaby for *years*. Every time I fell down in the playground or had something fall on my head, you were there to laugh and say something mean. You try to scare me every day. And why? Just to make your

dopey friends laugh."

"Well, that's true," I admitted. "But I can explain that—"

"No!" the ghost of Emily shouted at me. "Now *I'm* going to do the explaining, A.J.! I know why you say mean things to me.

It's because you're an immature, obnoxious, and insecure little boy."

"I am not!" I shouted. "Stop saying mean things to me!"

"No!" the ghost of Emily shouted in my face. "You're mean to my best friend, Andrea, all the time too. And I know why. It's to disguise the fact that you are secretly in love with her! Ha! There, I said it!"

"I am *not* in love with Andrea!" I shouted.

"Liar!" the ghost of Emily yelled. "Admit it! You're a liar and a hater! And not only that, but you're . . . a dumbhead!"

WHAT?! I can't believe she called me the *D* word. That's like the worst thing you can say to anybody. I felt tears gathering in the corners of my eyes.

"Are you crying, A.J.?" the ghost of Emily said. "Is that a tear I see? Well, I guess the shoe is on the other foot *now*, isn't it, A.J.?"

"Why would I put my shoes on the wrong feet?" I whimpered, wiping my eyes. "What do shoes have to do with anything?"

"Don't play dumb, A.J.," shouted the ghost of Emily. "Being made fun of isn't much fun when people are making fun of *you*, now is it?"

"Stop! Leave me alone!" I shouted.

"Oh, I'll leave you alone," said the ghost of Emily. "*Everybody* is going to leave you alone this summer. So nah-nah-nah boo-boo on you! How does it feel? How does it feel to be on your own, with no direction home, like a complete unknown?"*

"It feels bad," I said, wiping my face with my sheet.

"You made me cry so many times, A.J.," the ghost of Emily said. "Well, who's crying *now*? You're going to have the worst summer of your life! I'll make sure of it! Good-BYE!"

The ghost of Emily made that eerie cackling laugh again and drifted out the window, like the other ghosts.

What a horrible night. Nothing could make this night any worse.

And then something happened that made the night even *worse*.

---

*Ask your parents, or maybe your grandparents.

The Ghost of Summers Yet to Come

The clock struck four. It was useless to try and go back to sleep. Soon it would be morning. Somehow, I'd survived. It was almost time to get up and go to school. And then . . .

"A.J. . . . A.J. . . . A.J. . . ."

Oh no. Not *another one.*

I heard a faraway rumbling sound. Scary music started to play. I didn't want to open my eyes to find out who or what I was going to encounter next. But I did anyway. I looked down and noticed that the floor of my room was covered in smoke. And then . . .

"Ahhhhhhhhhh!"

It was a dark, hooded figure floating over my bed. I couldn't see its face. I didn't *want* to see its face. It was sure to be terrifying.

And then the scary figure spoke.

"Come . . . with . . . me, . . . Arlo."

Wait. Arlo? There's only one person in

the world that calls me by my real name. Even my *parents* don't call me Arlo. It had to be . . .

Andrea Young!

It couldn't be true! Not Andrea! Not after everything I had already been through!

"You sound like Andrea," I whispered, shrinking back in terror.

"That's because I *am* Andrea!" she shouted, pulling the hood away from her face. She let out an eerie cackling laugh.

"Ahhhhhhhhhh!" I screamed. "Mom! Dad! Help!"

"Your parents can't hear you, Arlo," the ghost of Andrea told me. "It's just you and me now."

"What do you want?" I asked, my voice quivering. "Leave me alone."

"I'm the ghost of summers yet to come, Arlo," the ghost of Andrea said in a spooky voice. "I'm here to show you your future."

"I don't *want* to see my future!" I screamed, gathering the covers around me. "Seeing the past was horrible. Seeing right now was horrible. I can't imagine how bad the future is going to be."

"Oh, the future is going to be *wonderful*, Arlo," the ghost of Andrea assured me.

"No, it won't," I said. "You're trying to trick me. And stop calling me Arlo."

"But that's your name," the ghost of Andrea said. "Come with me, Arlo."

"No."

I folded my hands across my chest, because that's what you do when you don't want to go anywhere. Nobody knows why.

"Arlo," the ghost of Andrea repeated, "come with me."

"No! No way!"

"I . . . said, . . . come . . . with . . . ME!"

"Ahhhhhhhhhh!"

The next thing I knew, the ghost of Andrea had grabbed my hand, yanked me out of bed, and shoved me out the window. We were flying. But I didn't want to fly anymore. Not with Andrea.

"Where are you taking me?" I asked as we floated over my house.

"Oh, you'll find out. Come on. We don't want to be late."

Late? Late for *what*?

We flew past some rooftops, and then Andrea made a right turn at the corner and swooped down toward the steeple of a church.

"Why are we going to church?" I asked.

"Why do you *think* we're going to church, Arlo?" the ghost of Andrea replied.

We glided inside the church. I looked down. All our teachers and the other grown-ups from Ella Mentry School were sitting in the pews. I could see Ms. Hannah, the art teacher. She was sitting next to Miss Lazar, the custodian. There was

Miss Holly, the Spanish teacher, and Mr. Tony, the after-school program director. Miss Klute, our therapy dog, was there. Even Ella Mentry was there, the old lady our school was named after. Everybody was all dressed up in their nicest clothes.

Standing in the front of all the pews and facing the crowd was Mayor Hubble, the mayor of our town. He was holding a book. There were two people standing in front of him. A boy and a girl. They were turned around so I couldn't tell who they were. The boy was wearing a black suit and the girl was wearing a long white gown.

Then I realized something. The boy and the girl . . . were me and Andrea!

*Ahhhhhhhhhh!** I couldn't even scream. The words were stuck in my throat. Andrea and I were about to be married!

"Isn't this romantic, Arlo?" asked the ghost of Andrea.

"No!"

"Dear friends," said Mayor Hubble, "we are gathered here today to celebrate the union of this woman, Andrea, and this man, A.J.—"

"Noooooooooooooo!" I hollered. "This can't be happening!"

"Oh, Arlo, don't be silly," the ghost of Andrea told me. "You knew this day would come. You and I were destined to be together. It's fate."

Ahhhhhhhhhh!

"Noooooooooooooo!"

The ghost of Andrea had a smile on her face. "Don't I look pretty down there in my wedding dress?" she asked. "And you look so handsome, Arlo."

"Noooooooooooooo!"

"In their years together," said Mayor Hubble, "A.J. and Andrea have come to realize that their personal hopes, goals, and dreams . . . blah blah blah blah . . . and so they have decided to live together as husband and wife."

"Noooooooooooooo! Please don't make me! I'll do *anything.*"

"In the future, you're going to grow up and become mature," the ghost of

Andrea told me. "You'll stop saying mean things and doing mean things to people. We're going to have nine children together, and they're all going to look like me."

"No! It can't be true!"

"Oh, calm down, Arlo," the ghost of Andrea told me. "We're going to live happily ever after, just like in the fairy tales."

"Noooooooooooooo!"

"Is there anyone here who has a reason why these two should not be joined in holy matrimony?" asked Mayor Hubble. "Speak now, or forever hold your peace."

"I DO!" I shouted at the top of my lungs. "ME! A.J.!"

"Anyone?" asked Mayor Hubble, looking around.

"ME!" I screamed again. "I have a big problem with this!"

"He can't hear you, Arlo," said the ghost of Andrea. "*Nobody* can hear you except me."

"Okay then," said Mayor Hubble. "Do you, Andrea, take this man to be your lawful husband, to have and to hold from this day forward, for better, for worse, for richer, for poorer, in sickness and in health, to love and to cherish . . . blah blah blah blah . . . till death do you part?"

"I do," Andrea said.

"Stop!" I screamed. "Make it go away!

Isn't there *anything* I can do? Does it have to be this way? Please don't make me get married to Andrea! I'm sorry for everything I ever did! I can change! I'll

be nicer! To everybody! I promise! Please? Forgive me! I just want to go to sleep! I'm too young to be married!"

"It's too late, Arlo," the ghost of Andrea told me. "There's nothing you can do to stop it. This is your future. We're going to have a summer wedding."

Mayor Hubble didn't hear anything we were saying.

"And do you, A.J., take this woman to be your wife, in sickness and in health . . . blah blah blah blah . . . till death do you part?"

"NO!" I shouted as loud I could. "I DON'T!"

"Wonderful!" said Mayor Hubble. "I

now pronounce you husband and wife. A.J., you may kiss the bride."

"Ahhhhhhhh! Noooooooooo! Help!"

The ghost of Andrea turned to me and let out another eerie cackling laugh. Then she made a kissy-face with her lips.

And then she leaned toward me.

The Next Day at School

That's all I remember. I woke up covered in sweat. The clock at my bedside said it was seven o'clock, which was weird because I never had a clock at my bedside. I wonder where that clock came from.

I looked around. Everything seemed normal. There was no evidence that all those ghosts had visited me during the night.

"A.J.!" my mom called from downstairs. "It's time to get up for school."

"I don't feel good, Mom," I said. "Can I stay home today?"

"Oh, you say that every day, silly!" my mother replied.

I dragged myself out of bed and got dressed. I went downstairs to eat breakfast and rode my bike to school.

The first person I saw when I got to class was Andrea. She was putting her backpack into her cubby.

"Good morning, Arlo," Andrea said cheerfully.

"Ahhhhhhhhhh!" I screamed in horror. "Don't touch me! Leave me alone!"

"What is *your* problem?" Andrea asked. "All I said was good morning."

I went over to the guys, hoping Andrea wouldn't follow me.

"Are you okay, dude?" Ryan asked me. "You look like you've seen a ghost."

"I *did*," I told him. "I feel sick. I think I

need to go to the nurse's office."

That's when the weirdest thing in the history of the world happened. Our school nurse, Mrs. Cooney, was walking by our classroom.

"Did somebody say the word 'sick'?" she asked excitedly. Mrs. Cooney loves it when kids get sick. If kids didn't get sick, she wouldn't have a job.

"A.J. thinks he's sick," said Michael.

Mrs. Cooney pulled a thermometer out of her pocket.

"Say *ah*," she said, poking the thermometer into my mouth.

It took a million hundred seconds for the thermometer to beep. Finally it did, and Mrs. Cooney looked at it.

"Ninety-eight point six," she said. "Perfectly normal. You're fine, A.J."

"Arlo is faking it," Andrea told Mrs. Cooney. "He just wants to get out of school. Arlo does that all the time. But he *is* really sick—sick in the *head*!"

"Oh, snap!" said Ryan. "Andrea said you're sick in the head! Are you gonna take that, A.J.?"

I looked at Andrea. She had her hands on her hips. When girls put their hands on their hips, it means they're mad. Nobody knows why.

"Aren't you going to say something mean back to Andrea?" asked Neil.

"Yeah, A.J.," said Michael. "Aren't you going to say something mean back to Andrea?"

I was faced with the hardest decision of my life. If I said something mean back to Andrea, I would get in trouble. And if I didn't say something mean back to Andrea, all the guys would say I was in love with her. Ryan was looking at me. Michael was looking at me. Neil was looking at me. Emily was looking at me. *Everybody* was looking at me.

It was so quiet, you could hear a pin drop.* I didn't know what to say. I didn't know what to do. I had to think fast.

"No," I said. "I'm not going to say something mean back to Andrea."

I went to my desk and sat down.

---

*Well, that is if anybody had brought pins with them. But who brings pins to school? That would be weird.

"Oooooh," Ryan said, "A.J. isn't going to say anything mean back to Andrea! He must be in *love* with her!"

"When are you gonna get married?" asked Michael.

Well, that's pretty much what happened. Maybe all those ghosts will stop bothering me and mind their own business. Maybe I'll get to fly again. Maybe Billy will stop running around in his underwear. Maybe the ghost will get out of our vacuum cleaner. Maybe the earth's rotation will slow down again so we can have summer this year. Maybe Dr. Brad will strap me to a chair and put a monkey brain in my skull. Maybe the ice cream shortage will end. Maybe I won't have to repeat first, second, and third grade. Maybe Emily will stop saying mean things to me. Maybe I won't have to marry Andrea. Maybe I'll get a good night's sleep again. Maybe I'll try to be a nicer person.

But it won't be easy!

MY WeiRd SchooL SpeciaL!

Bummer in the Summer!

WEIRD EXTRAS!

★ Professor A.J.'s Weird Summer Facts

★ Fun Games and Weird Word Puzzles

★ My Weird School Trivia Questions

PROFESSOR A.J.'S WEIRD SUMMER FACTS

Howdy, fellow weirdos! This is your old pal Professor A.J., speaking to you from my secret laboratory hidden in an abandoned warehouse on the outskirts of town. I've been hiding here ever since I found out that I'll have to marry Andrea someday. She'll never find me here.

Since I'm in the gifted and talented program at school, I know lots of stuff that normal kids don't know. Today I'm going to tell you about my favorite time of year: summer.

Summer started a long, long time ago, back in 1976. Before that year, there was no summer. It's true. People went from spring right into winter. It was a sad time. Everybody was depressed. Kids were crying all the time. Nobody knew what to do about it. And then this guy named Bob Summer came up with the idea of sticking a new season between spring and winter. Everybody thought he was a genius, and they named the new season after Bob Summer. If you ask me, they should have called the new season Bob. So then the seasons would be winter, spring, fall, and Bob. But anyway, Bob Summer won the Nobel Prize for coming up with the idea. That's a prize they give out to people who don't have bells. And that, my friends, is how summer was born.

Arlo, you totally made that up!

Eeeeek! It's Andrea! Who let you in here?

Don't you remember? We're supposed to write this part of the book *together*. So here's some real *true* stuff about summer that most people probably don't know. . . .

You've heard of the Eiffel Tower in Paris? Well, it's made of iron. In the summer, the iron gets hot and it expands. So the tower is more than six inches taller in the summer than it is in the winter.

What?! Get out of here! That can't be true! You made that up.

It's true, Arlo. If you don't believe me, look it up.

Oh, yeah. Well, I can top that summer fact. Try this one on for size—an eleven-year-old kid invented ice pops.

Very funny, Arlo.

It's true.

No way!

Yes way! His name was Frank Epperson, and he lived in the San Francisco Bay Area. One night during the winter of 1905, he was fooling around with some sugary soda powder. He mixed it with water and stirred it up. Then he accidentally left it outside with the stirring stick in it. In the morning, the liquid was frozen, and Epperson had the first ice pop in the history of the world.

How could you possibly know that, Arlo?

I happen to know a lot about ice pops, okay? Epperson named his new invention the Epsicle and started selling it to the kids in his neighborhood.

I get it—he combined "Epperson" and "icicle" to get "Epsicle." So where did the name Popsicle come from?

Epperson waited almost twenty years to get a patent for his invention. It was his own children who convinced him to change the name. It was their "Pop's

'Sicle," so it became the "Popsicle."

That sounds a lot like one of your ridiculous stories, Arlo.

Don't believe me? Here's Frank Epperson's patent. . . .

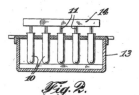

Aug. 19 , 1924.

F. W. EPPERSON

1,505,592

FROZEN CONFECTIONERY

Original Filed June 11 , 1924

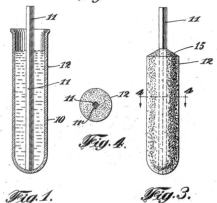

INVENTOR
Frank W. Epperson
BY
Dean Fairbank Knight & Hirsch
his ATTORNEYS

Wow! Maybe I underestimated you, Arlo. But let me ask you this. What exactly *is* summer?

Huh? Any dumbhead knows what summer is. Summer is when you eat Popsicles.

You can eat Popsicles *any* time of year! Did you know that when it's summer in the Northern Hemisphere, it's winter in the Southern Hemisphere?

Of course I know that. Everybody knows that. What's a hemisphere?

You really don't know *anything* about summer, do you? A "sphere" is a ball, like the earth. Hemi means "half." So a hemisphere is half of the earth. There's a Northern Hemisphere, where we live, and a Southern Hemisphere. The equator separates the two hemispheres.

I knew all that. I was just yanking your chain. In the Northern Hemisphere, summer goes from June to August. In the Southern Hemisphere, it's from December to February. For us, summer begins around June 21 and ends around September 23.

Everybody knows it's hotter in the summer than in the winter. But do you know *why* it's hotter, Arlo?

Because the earth is closer to the sun in the summer?

That's what a lot of people *think*. Actually, it's the opposite! The earth is *farther* from the sun during our summer.

Then why does it get hot in the summer?

It's all because of the way the earth is tilted toward the sun.

The earth is tilted? Stop the world! I want to get off!

Very funny, Arlo. The earth is tilted all the time, and it doesn't change as we orbit around the sun. So when the Northern Hemisphere is tilted toward the sun, the sun's rays hit that part of the planet more directly than at any other time of the year, and it's hotter. Then, six months later, the Northern Hemisphere has tilted *away* from the sun. The sun's rays don't hit it so directly, so it's colder and we have winter. And it's the exact opposite for the Southern Hemisphere.

I knew all that stuff.

You did not.

Did too.

Let's just agree to disagree, okay?

I disagree with that.

Here are a few more cool facts about the summer. . . .

Did you ever hear the expression "the dog days of summer"? Those are the weeks between July 3 and August 11. They're named after Sirius, the Dog Star. In ancient Greece, people blamed Sirius for the heat, drought, and sickness that arrived every summer.

Did you ever wonder where the months got their names?

Well, I know how they named the month of May. In ancient times, they didn't have calendars, so people were never sure what day it was. They were really confused all the time. Sometimes they forgot all about the month that came after April and the one that came before June. So they named it May because it may or may not come each year.

That's ridiculous, Arlo! You made that whole thing up!

Yeah, but it sounds good, doesn't it?

I'll tell you how they *really* named the summer months. June was named after either Juniores, the lower branch of the Roman Senate, or Juno, the wife of Jupiter. The Roman general Marc Antony named July in honor of Julius Caesar. And Caesar's adopted nephew Gaius Julius Caesar Octavius named August after himself. He held the title Augustus. You've got to have a lot of nerve to name a month after yourself.

If you ask me, they should name a month Arlo.

It's too late. All the months are taken.

Well, they should start a new month and name it Arlo.

You can't just start a new month, dumbhead! That's not how it works. Let's talk about summer foods. My favorite is watermelon. Did you know that watermelon isn't a fruit? Technically, it's a vegetable. It's part of the cucumber, pumpkin, and squash family.

Squashes have families? That must be interesting at Thanksgiving time. What do they do, sit on each other?

Very funny, Arlo. You probably also don't

know that 92 percent of a watermelon is water.

And the other 8 percent must be melon, so it has the perfect name.

On average, Americans consume more than fifteen pounds of watermelon a year.

And that's not to mention all the watermelon that gets squashed during Thanksgiving.

Speaking of summer foods, July is National Ice Cream Month. The average American eats about twenty quarts of ice cream a year. But that's just the average. I think I eat twenty quarts of ice cream a *day*.

Do you know what the most popular ice cream flavor is, Arlo?

Banana bubblegum nut crunch surprise?

No, vanilla.

That was my next guess.

According to *Rolling Stone* magazine, the best summer song of all time is "Dancing in the Street" by Martha and the Vandellas.*

---

*What's a Vandella? Nobody knows.

The world record for the most people applying sunscreen at one time was set on January 8, 2012 in Australia. Over a thousand people put on sunscreen for two minutes. That proves two things—there are too many world records, and Australians have too much time on their hands.

Here's something most people don't know. Before the Civil War, kids didn't get a summer vacation from school.

What?! No way! That's not fair! Bummer in the summer for them!

It's true. Many families lived on farms back then, and the kids were needed during the spring and fall to work in the fields, so school in those areas took place in winter and summer. It wasn't until the twentieth century that kids got off from school for the summer.

Okay, that's all I know about summer. Professor A.J. out.

And this is Andrea Young. I'm going to Harvard someday. Have a great summer!

FUN GAMES AND WEIRD WORD PUZZLES

SCHOOL'S OUT WORD SEARCH

Directions: The school year is finally over for A.J. and the gang! Can you find the ten things that would make this summer a total bummer?

```
C N I G H T M A R E X E O Y H
Z V Z H A J X D V A Z G P M M
U G R O W N U P S X T I W E A
T V H O M E W O R K X D X K T
E G Z J J K T L C V W F P B H
N C R H V M V D L W Z S S O V
T E A C H E R W G C I G B B F
D U B G U G I R H U N O O D H
G U L H D H W X O Z B G O Z X
B S K O R U L E S U K V K I S
W I V T S Z U M T A C V S T K
L W C I D O X E S Y T Z M W I
O Q I G H Y P E I J D H N Y B
V Z T E S T S V Z V P K U G Y
E R X J K C O Q C A C K L E S
```

NIGHTMARE   HOMEWORK
TEACHER   RULES   GHOSTS
GROWNUPS   TESTS
BOOKS   LOVE   MATH

SUMMER, SET, MATCH!

Directions: Each of the words or phrases in the list below matches one of the words in bold. See if you can pair them up!

Video → _____

Ice → _____

Ping- → _____

Peace → _____

Beach → _____

Summer → _____

Fairy → _____

Holy → _____

Swimming → _____

PONG

CREAM

POOL

SIGN

HOUSE

TALE

GAMES

READING

MATRIMONY

SUMMER WORD JUMBLE:

Directions: Unscramble the letters below to find out why A.J. and Andrea think summer is the most wonderful time of the year.

WLAEMRENTO: _____

NCAEO: _____

RISEFBE: _____

OBLUAWGN: _____

ELCROO: _____

PESEL: _____

UFN: _____

WORDS YET TO COME

Directions: Words can do weird things when you scramble them! See how many smaller words you can make from the letters in these bigger words. Try to come up with at least ten new, smaller words for each! Here's an example:

MY WEIRD SCHOOL

1. Loom   **2. Cool**   **3. Dries**

SUMMER VACATION	NORTHERN HEMISPHERE	SAND CASTLE
1	1	1
2	2	2
3	3	3
4	4	4
5	5	5
6	6	6
7	7	7
8	8	8
9	9	9
10	10	10

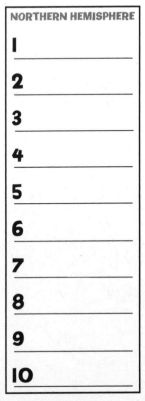
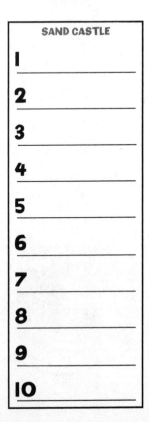

SPOT THE DIFFERENCES

Directions: These two covers are identical. Well, *almost*. There are six differences. Can you spot them?

MY WEIRD SCHOOL TRIVIA

There's no way in a million hundred years you'll get all these answers right. So nah-nah-nah boo-boo on you! (Hint: all the answers to the questions below come from the My Weird School Specials, including this one.)

TRIVIA QUESTIONS:

Q: IF A.J. COULD HAVE ONE SUPERPOWER, WHAT WOULD IT BE?

A: To fly

Q: WHAT DID A.J. AND THE GANG START CALLING THEIR CAFETERIA AFTER A FIRST GRADER THREW UP IN IT?

A: The vomitorium

Q: WHAT'S A.J.'S FAVORITE HOLIDAY?

A: Halloween

Q: WHO DOES ANDREA WANT TO MARRY AND BUILD SAND CASTLES WITH?

A: Mr. Sunny

Q: WHAT TYPE OF ANIMAL DOES MISS MARY KEEP AS A PET?

A: A bat

Q: WHO INVENTED THE POPSICLE?

A: Frank Epperson

Q: WHAT SEPARATES THE NORTHERN AND SOUTHERN HEMISPHERES?

A: Billy

Q: WHICH OF A.J.'S FRIENDS LIVES AROUND THE CORNER FROM HIM BUT GOES TO ANOTHER SCHOOL?

A: The equator

Q: WHO TRIED TO STEAL THE BURGER QUEEN GOLDEN EASTER EGG?

A: Mayor Hubble and his wife, Bubbles Hubble

Q: WHAT SWEET TREAT IS A.J. MOST LOOKING FORWARD TO ON EASTER?

A: Peeps

Q: WHAT REWARD DOES A.J. GET FOR RECITING THE EIGHT TIMES TABLE FOR MR. KLUTZ?

A: He gets to dye Mr. Klutz's head!

Q: WHAT LANGUAGE DO MS. LAGRANGE AND PIERRE SPEAK?

A: French

Q: WHAT SHOULD WE CELEBRATE ON VALENTINE'S DAY?

A: Tolerance, acceptance, and love in the world

Q: WHO IS DRESSED AS FROSTY THE SNOWMAN IN SANTA'S WORKSHOP?

A: Miss Lazar

Q: WHAT DOES A.J. WANT EVERY YEAR FOR CHRISTMAS?

A: A new Striker Smith action figure

Q: WHAT IS MS. HANNAH'S FAVORITE COLOR?

A: Green

Q: WHAT SORT OF PRANKS DO MOST KIDS PULL ON MISCHIEF NIGHT?

A: They throw eggs, soap up windows, ring doorbells, and cover trees with toilet paper!

Q: HOW DOES A.J. KNOW HIS PARENTS WILL AGREE TO JUST ABOUT ANYTHING?

A: They rub their foreheads with their fingers.

Q: WHAT TIME DO KIDS START TRICK-OR-TREATING IN A.J.'S TOWN?

A: Four o'clock in the afternoon

Q: MRS. YONKERS HAS HER OWN COMPUTER COMPANY CALLED NERD. WHAT DOES NERD STAND FOR?

A: New Electronic Research Development

ANSWER KEY:

SCHOOL'S OUT WORD SEARCH

```
C  N  I  G  H  T  M  A  R  E  X  E  O  Y  H
Z  V  Z  H  A  J  X  D  V  A  Z  G  P  M  M
U  G  R  O  W  N  U  P  S  X  T  I  W  E  A
T  V  H  O  M  E  W  O  R  K  X  D  X  K  T
E  G  Z  J  J  K  T  L  C  V  W  F  P  B  H
N  C  R  H  V  M  V  D  L  W  Z  S  S  O  V
D  T  E  A  C  H  E  R  W  G  C  I  G  B  B  F
D  U  B  G  U  G  I  R  H  U  N  O  O  D  H
G  U  L  H  D  H  W  X  O  Z  B  G  O  Z  X
B  S  K  O  R  U  L  E  S  U  K  V  K  I  S
W  I  V  T  S  Z  U  M  T  A  C  V  S  T  K
L  W  C  I  D  O  X  E  S  Y  T  Z  M  W  I
O  Q  I  G  H  Y  P  E  I  J  D  H  N  Y  B
V  Z  T  E  S  T  S  V  Z  V  P  K  U  G  Y
E  R  X  J  K  C  O  Q  C  A  C  K  L  E  S
```

SUMMER SET MATCH!

Video → Games
Ice → Cream
Ping- → Pong
Peace → Sign
Beach → House
Summer → Reading
Fairy → Tale
Holy → Matrimony
Swimming → Pool

SUMMER WORD JUMBLE:

WLAEMRENTO: WATERMELON
NCAEO: OCEAN
RISEFBE: FRISBEE
OBLUAWGN: BUNGALOW
ELCROO: COOLER
PESEL: SLEEP
UFN: FUN

WORDS YET TO COME

**Here are just a few of the many words you may
have found!**

SUMMER VACATION	NORTHERN HEMISPHERE	SAND CASTLE
1 CAT	1 TORN	1 DANCE
2 IN	2 PIER	2 LEAN
3 NOT	3 HIM	3 TEND
4 MAT	4 THERE	4 STAND
5 SUN	5 ROT	5 DENT
6 RATION	6 RENT	6 LAND
7 SOME	7 EERIE	7 LASS
8 MOM	8 SPENT	8 END
9 CAST	9 TREE	9 CANDLE
10 EARN	10 OTHER	10 LEAST

SPOT THE DIFFERENCES